SpongeBob SquarePants
NICKELODEON

# The Song That Never Ends

by Steven Banks
illustrated by Vince DePorter

## SCHOLASTIC INC.

New York   Toronto   London   Auckland   Sydney
Mexico City   New Delhi   Hong Kong   Buenos Aires

D0465728

*Stephen Hillenburg*

Based on the TV series *SpongeBob SquarePants*® created by Stephen Hillenburg
as seen on Nickelodeon®

ISBN 0-439-59886-9

12 11 10 9 8 7 6 5 4 3 2                    4 5 6 7 8 9/0

Printed in China

First Schoalstic Printing, May 2004

SpongeBob SquarePants and his friend Patrick heard strange noises coming from their neighbor Squidward's house.
"Out!" shouted Squidward.
"Out, I say!"

"Squidward is in trouble!"
said SpongeBob.
"Call the police!"

Patrick started running in a circle
and yelling, "Police! Police!"
SpongeBob ran to Squidward's house.

Squidward was throwing things away
in a trash can. "Out with it all!"
"I will save you!" shouted SpongeBob.
"From what?" asked Squidward.
"I am just cleaning out my closet."

"Oh, I thought you were in trouble,"
said SpongeBob.
Squidward sighed. "The only trouble
I have is you bothering me!
Now, leave me alone so I can finish!"

Patrick ran in with a policeman.
"What's the problem here?"
asked the officer.
"No problem, officer,"
said Squidward.
"So why did you need me?"
the policeman demanded.

"I did not!" complained Squidward.
"Then do not waste my time!"
 said the policeman.
"I have my eye on you, Squidward!"

SpongeBob looked in Squidward's
trash can and saw a little toy guitar.
"Why are you throwing this away?"
he asked.
"It's just an old toy I played with
when I was a kid," said Squidward.

"It's broken, but it used to play
a silly little song."
"Can I have it?" asked SpongeBob.
"Sure," said Squidward. "It's a
worthless piece of junk!"

"Thank you, Squidward!"
said SpongeBob. "If you ever want
to visit your guitar,
just drop in anytime."
"Fine, SpongeBob," said Squidward.
"I will keep that in mind. Now go."

SpongeBob popped his head in
Squidward's window.
"If you change your mind
it will be right next door!
You know where to find us!"
"GO AWAY!" yelled Squidward.

When SpongeBob and Patrick got home,
SpongeBob fixed the toy guitar.
He turned the crank
and out came music.
"What a beautiful song,"
said SpongeBob.

"I could listen to it all day long!"
"Me too!" agreed Patrick.
    So they did.

Squidward stuck his head
out the window. "SpongeBob!
Stop playing that song!
It's driving me crazy!"

"Okay, Squidward," said SpongeBob.
"I'll stop for today."

"But I want a turn!"
complained Patrick.
SpongeBob handed him
the little guitar.

"You can play the song one more time."
Patrick was so excited, he turned the crank too hard and it broke off. But the song kept playing!

Squidward banged on SpongeBob's door.
"I said, stop playing that song!"

SpongeBob tried as hard as he could,
but he could not stop the song.
"I am calling the police!"
Squidward shouted.

"What now?" asked the policeman.
"Arrest this sponge and stop
   that song!" demanded Squidward.
"I like that song," said the
   policeman. "My mother used to hum it
   when she tucked me in at night.
   SpongeBob, you can play that song
   as much as you like!"

The song kept playing all night long.
Squidward put a pillow over his head,
but he could still hear it.
"I can't take it anymore!"
said Squidward. "I have got to stop
that song once and for all!"

Squidward quietly snuck into SpongeBob's house. SpongeBob was sound asleep, holding the guitar in his hands.
Squidward grabbed the guitar and SpongeBob woke up.

"Squidward, what are you doing?"
"Uh, nothing," replied Squidward.
SpongeBob smiled.

"I understand. You miss your little guitar. You were only pretending to hate the song. Here. Take it."

"I fooled SpongeBob!"
shouted Squidward as he ran outside.
Squidward raised the guitar in
the air and smashed it on a rock!
*Smash! Smash! Smash!*
The song finally stopped.
"I did it!" cried Squidward.

SpongeBob ran out and looked at
the busted guitar.

"Squidward, you destroyed that poor,
helpless guitar. What did it
ever do to you?"

"It kept playing that horrible song!"
said Squidward. "Now I never have
to hear it again! Ever!"

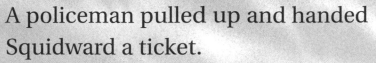

A policeman pulled up and handed
Squidward a ticket.
"It's against the law to smash a
guitar at two in the morning!
You are disturbing the peace!
That's a one-hundred-dollar fine!"

Just then a man appeared.
"My name is Fender Gibson. I collect
rare toy guitars. I thought you
might like to know that you just
smashed a one-of-a-kind
Straticastius guitar that would have
been worth a million dollars!"

R.I.P.
Guitar

"Look, Squidward!" said SpongeBob.
"I found the music box
   that plays the song!"
He turned the crank. "It still works!
You do not have a million dollars,
   but the song will play forever!"
"NOOOO!" screamed Squidward
   as he ran away.